AF138745

Author Vanessa Araya writes stories and novels about her protagonist, Juni Shimata, a character with a dissociative identity disorder. Vanessa Araya was born and raised in Gardena, California. She studied and taught music in California and is now retired. In 2008, Araya began writing as part of her attempts to come to terms with her own dissociative disorder.

Autorin Vanessa Araya schreibt Geschichten und Romane über die Abenteuer ihrer Protagonistin, Juni Shimata, die an einer dissoziativen Identitätsstörung leidet. Vanessa Araya ist in Gardena (Kalifornien) geboren und aufgewachsen. Sie studierte und unterrichtete dort Musik und ist jetzt Rentnerin. 2008 hat Araya als Therapie für ihre eigene dissoziative Störung zu schreiben begonnen.

Vanessa Araya

ROAD GIRL

A Story

FSC
www.fsc.org

MIX

Papier aus ver-
antwortungsvollen
Quellen
Paper from
responsible sources

FSC® C105338

©Vanessa Araya 2014
German version by Vanessa Araya
vanessa@junishimata.com
Cover photo from Vanessa's father's collection

Corrections by Dorothée Leidig, www.textsieben.de
Publication by Lektorat-Bär, www.lektorat-baer.de
ch@lektorat-baer.de
Stuttgart, Germany
Herstellung und Verlag:
BoD - Books on Demand, Norderstedt
ISBN 978-3-732-29984-3

Contents

MOMMY BY THE KITCHEN RADIO crying. Mommy never cries. "Mommy! What's the matter?"

About 5:15 p.m. Saturday she had called the psychiatrist, Dr. Ralph Greenson, and was told to go for a ride when she complained she could not sleep, police reported.

Sometimes Mommy tells the story about when her daddy died and then her mommy. Sometimes she cries.

Dr. Greenson took a poker from the fireplace, smashed in a window and climbed into the room. He told Det. Sgt. R. E. Byron that Miss Monroe was under a sheet and champagne-colored blanket which were tucked up around her shoulders.

"I don't know, angel. It just makes me feel s-s-o sad ... so a-alone."

So many tears! Mommy's hair is blond in front. Called peroxide. Blond curl up there like a little conch shell above her wet face.

"I'll be ok, sweetheart." She blows her nose. "Let's get back to work. We don't have any time to waste! Did you get your wool skirts out of the cedar chest?"

See-der-chest. The wooden chest from back home that smells strong. Prevents moths. "It's too hot for wool skirts today!"

"I'll put an LP on the hi-fi to cheer us up. How about Brubeck's *Take Five...*"

So hot. Better in the shady bedroom where the Venetian blinds are always drawn. Or on the tile floor in the bathroom. Silverfish in the corners. Back to school soon.

"Come on, Salvation Army is picking up old clothes next week, and the weekend after that is shopping in Bevrlyills with Connie so sort out your old skirts to make room. Geta move on! The sitter's coming in three hours and I have to do my hair!"

"Is Connie gonna sew something for *me* this time?"

"I already explained you that. You're too young and growing too fast. It's not worth ... investing so much in your clothes because you grow out of them so fast, but she'll coordinate the colors and put reinforcements in the pleats of your skirts so they'll hang better."

Hang better? "Mom, the phone's ringing."

"Go answer it, it might be your father. I need to talk to him. Hello, Jay? Juni, go play in your room while I talk with your father."

In solitaire, you lay out the cards, then turn up three at a time. Three at a time. Black goes on red, red goes on black. You build up on the aces. King goes on a free space. Sometimes you win without cheating but hardly ever.

And that was our Saturday morning concert here on KPFK, your non-affiliated Pacifica station in Los Angeles, broadcasting with 75,000 watts from Mount Wilson, featuring works by Mozart, Beethoven and Brahms.

Mommy moves her leg over the pedal called clutch. "Connie, did I tell you the girls from the office are planning a trip to Las Vegas in the fall?"

"Mmmm mmmm, yes, dear. Will you be needing any new clothes for the trip? I've seen some very short skirts this season, think they call them mini-skirts."

"With *my* knees?"

"Well, how about pants, being tall as you are ... you know, Courrèges left Balenciaga and opened his new house with a trouser suit this fall, I have some beautiful turquoise raw silk samples that would bring out your eyes – we could look for fabric at Magnin's."

Old Connie's hair falls down and she pins it up again. She's fat and has B.O. Clutch, gas, look-in-the-mirror. The bad car smell. Like gas stations. "How much longer till we get there? I'm getting carsick."

And now it's music from the Salzburg Festival with Verdi's Requiem Mass and Hurburt van Kra - jan conducting the Berlin Philharmonic.

"The Long Beach Freeway. Long Beach Boulevard, exiting on your right. Ladies and gentlemen, Compton Boulevard, exiting in 2 miles on the right. Merge left, exiting on the right. Imperial Highway, exiting in 4½ miles. Merge left, please…"

"Juni, stop that nonsense!"

"I'm just being a radio announcer and announcing the exits."

"Be still! I have to concentrate on driving."

"Balenciaga's fitted suit does well on you, but you didn't like his sack dress," Connie says. "The tailored Chanel look is better for you. And did I tell you, *Vogue* has a new editor – it's a woman."

"I'm thinking about getting a new car. I've had this old Ford ever since we moved into the house seven years ago."

Connie's two front teeth are fuzzy and red from lipstick. Her tongue moves over them and makes the smacking noise. "But chr car's colors are still so nice, what with the roof being red and the rest grey and all …"

"This old Mainline, there's a cute new model called the Falcon, have you see the ads, maybe Juni's father will buy it for us."

"The Hollywood Freeway. Please merge, ladies and gentlemen, off to your right. The two right lanes exit to the Hollywood Freeway ..."

"Juni, what did I say! Do I have to pull over and count to three? And what about your seat belt – why isn't it fastened? How many times do I have to tell you!"

Connie stares straight ahead at the freeway.

"But it hurts my tummy. I have a *tummy* ache!"

"Azure, we are going to Bullock's first, aren't we?"

"Yes, Connie, this is Wilshire."

A Negro man in a uniform comes to park the car. Mommy says that Negros are like Caucasians except they smell different.

"Here you are, and keep the change."

"Goodness gracious, Juni, Labor Day weekend is almost over, school starts on Tuesday! Are your blouses all ironed? You can stay up late and watch *Bonanza*."

We have a new ironing board that's a-jus-tible. You can make it lower. With my glasses, I can watch TV ironing. Little Joe is best, Hoss is creepy. You put distilled water into the iron, set the dial to cotton, and push the steam button. First you do the collar, wrong side, then right side. Ironing-blouses smell. Sweet. Soapy. Toasty. Ironing wool smells like poo-poo. Sometimes when Mommy irons, she does a foof and giggles. She says foof is short for foo-foo in Japanese, but she is Caucasian. Daddy is Japanese and he calls it a fart. Then you iron the shoulders, cuffs and sleeves. Last the body. That way the blouse doesn't get wrinkled. "I did the pink one and the short-sleeved white one."

"Well, do the long-sleeved white one and the light blue one, then you'll be set for the whole week. And tomorrow you can polish your shoes."

"Hurry up, Juni! Did you wash your face and brush your teeth? Did you pack your lunch pail and fill your thermos with milk? Let's go, you don't want to be late on the first day of school! Get in the back seat and fasten that seatbelt. No messing around with it, little lady! I'm going in with you today, I have to talk with your teacher. Go on over and stash your lunch pail away. Hello, Mrs. Mader, I'm Juni's mother, Mrs. Shimata."

"... so good in languages ... always questions ... too far ahead ..."

In fourth grade you go to a different building with Mrs. Mader. Mrs. Mader is wrinkled and soft and round. Powdery. Pale red hair. You can see the skin on her head. Room with a low ceiling. Stuffy. Out the window the hot asphalt playground and sandbox. Blue sky and clouds. In Mrs. Mader's class we have a big geography book and we read about Egypt and Sinai. She says the Prince of England is our age. Maybe we can marry him if we're pretty. We learn some more Spanish words. *Quiero comer. ¿Que hora es?* Every day after school I stay till Mommy comes and picks me up. Sometimes it gets dark. We play Bombs Over Tokyo. I am Tokyo. They throw the bombs. It takes a long time to drive home. There's traffic and Mommy uses the clutch. I get carsick.

"Don't think about it, Juni, just listen to the radio. It'll go away."

Our leadership in science and in industry, our hopes for peace and security, our obligations to ourselves as well as others, all require us to make this effort, to solve these mysteries, to solve them for the good of all men, and to become the world's leading space-faring nation.

"Did you hear what the President said, Juni? We're in a space race with Russia, and we want to win. You could help. Do you want to learn Russian?"

Regina is retarded. Regina is a funny name because it sounds like vagina. She's in the fifth grade but she's fourteen. She's taller than everyone else and she has her period. She always has a special bag with stuff she leaves by the coat rack. Sometimes she smells fishy. Her glasses make her eyes look big. Pink plastic frames up in the corners with tiny rhinestones. Regina helped me the day I started in first grade. Mommy always tells me that. Mommy used to be a soshal worker. She was a caseworker. Sometimes I drove with her when she had to do field work. She held the folders tight and smiled at the Negros and showed her teeth and looked down and nodded her head. Now she's a secretary at Raytheon and she stands up straight and she always tucks her fanny under. Regina always wears the same red plaid skirt. Not cute. The pleats don't hang right. She's weird. I don't talk to her anymore. Once Joe Bell said damm and Mr. Church put borax from the boys' restroom in his mouth and Joe ran around for 20 minutes with his mouth wide open and he had big eyes and was scared. But we heard Mr. Church cuss too. Once in the shade on the asphalt Larry and I said we would show each other ours so I showed Larry mine like I did at Daddy's but Larry didn't show me his and Mr. Church found out. So what? Mommy didn't care but Mr. Church made me hurt.

"Anyway, Juni, I discussed it with your father, and you don't have to spend weekends there anymore. He'll come visit you Wednesdays after school, you hear? He'll park in front of the school and wait for you. Ok?"

14

That's his silver Cadillac.

It has the biggest tail fins of all. It says Sixty Special on the side in cursive, like we learned last year in penmanship, and Fleetwood on the back in capital letters. It has a special made headrest because Daddy has a whip lash and has to wear a scarf on his neck all the time. Once cousin Akiko got her period in the back seat and didn't say anything so there was blood on the grey seat-cover you can still see and Daddy put a wet sponge on it for a week and kept rubbing it and said Stupid Girl. But usually he likes her tee-tees. Mommy says breasts or bust but we say tee-tees. Daddy's car is messy and filled with junk. Just like his house. Lotsa rubbers, dental floss all over the place because we have to floss our teeth every day, the gun with the white handle, the *zafu* Granma made for when he meditates, his stethoscope and beenoculars and bongos, oranges because Daddy told me about his dream he made a serum out of oranges and saved Granpa's life and because he had to pick oranges when he was a kid on the farm in Riverside, the Exakta and the Asahi Pentax and the brown leather camera case and lotsa rolls a film all over and lotsa pens and paper and sketch books and plays and scripts to learn. And his brown corduroy jacket. I'm

15

not allowed to touch the gun but Daddy lets me play with the rubbers. They smell like everything else made out of rubber like the ball at school. There's the ones in the little flat wrappers like a piece of gum that say Trojan-Enz and the ones in the little blue plastic boxes with Japanese letters on them. I roll them out and blow them up and then I have rubber and talcum on my lips. And he makes me read the scripts with him. I have to play the roles like last year in the play when I sang on stage every night in Morgan Hall on Locust Street near school and I got to wear a dark red velvet cape and a crown and I held a septer and Joe Bell who used to go to reform school did a tap dance in front of me and everybody said you couldn't hear my song because he was so loud and Daddy took about a million pictures.

From thc Cadillac, music.

Before we continue with our top ten, let's hear the slow version of last month's hit by Neil Sedaka – here it is!

Doo-doo-doo
Down doobie-doo down-down, kamma kamma
Girl there's just no livin'
With-ou-ou-out you...

The driver, gazing at Juni.

16

Here she comes, my Juni-chan. New glasses thick as mine, poor kid. Getting to be a Big Girl. Got to explain her a few things ...

Don't take you-ur love away from me
Re-mem-ber whe-en you held me tight
And you kissed me all throooough the night

"Hey, kiddo, waddayaknow? So ya don wanna spend weekends with me anymore, huh. Well, gimme a kiss anyway. Wadya do in school tday?"

"Mrs. Mader and geography."

"I wanna teachya a cuppla things tday, too, ok?"

Eye-roll.

"Looka here ... where's my sketchpad ... This here's a man, ok? An ya know, he has a penis."

Like always.

"An insida him he's got these little tiny things that swim around call sperm, ya see? An this here's a lady an insida her she's got an egg, called an oh-vum."

So what?

"When a sperm meets the egg it's called fer-ti-li-za-tion and then the egg starts to divide, like this:

First in two, then in four, and so on. See what I mean? Until all the cells of a baby are made, like baby Juni."

"Daddy, where're we gonna eat tonight?"

"Naw, com-on, this's importan, I wancha t'pay attention. An before she can produce an egg, the lady has to menstruate."

"Yeah I know but I'm hun - gry."

"Well, didja unnerstand?"

"The man has the penis and the sperms and the lady has the egg and she has to men-yu-strate and then the egg divides and makes the baby."

"Men-stru-ate. Ok, well ifya wanna we cud go to the bay and I'll take a swim an then we cn eat fish sticks."

"With tartar sauce?"

"Yeah."

"O boy fish sticks – let's go!"

And now we continue our top ten countdown with this week's number one from the Four Seasons!

Sher-er-rry, Sherry baby
I'm gonna make-a you mi-yi-yi-ine

Juni and her mother are driving home from school in their Ford.

In related activity, more than 1,000 Czechoslovaks protested the U.S. arms blockade against Cuba in front of the U.S. Embassy in Prague chanting 'Yankee go home'.

"I'm carsick."

"Think of something else, Juni. Your father's coming tonight. It's been two weeks since he's seen you, and he's coming tonight to pick you up."

"Tonight? To make up for not coming yesterday?"

"No, he's going to take you on a trip."

"But tomorrow's Friday. If he takes me on a trip now I'll miss school. Anyway I thought I didn't have to spend weekends with him anymore."

"This time is special. You need to pack your things. You'll be staying away for several days."

"Where are we going? Do I have to get shots like when he went to Japan? If I have to get a shot I'm not going!"

"No shots, settle down. Maybe you'll drive out to the desert. It'll be a surprise."

"How come everything always has to be a surprise with Daddy? Do I get to skip ballet?"

"Yes."

"Oh goodie!" I hate ballet and old Mrs. Lebedeff pokes my bottom with a stick.

"You haven't seen your father since his birthday. You can bake him a cake or something if you do it quickly."

"Can I make strawberry shortcake?"

19

"If you want. Look, we're just by McDaniel's market. You run and get a can of whipped cream, and I'll get the strawberries. Meet you at the cashier's in two shakes of a sheep's tail ..."

"... No, she's not! I gave birth to her myself!"

"What's the matter, Mommy?"

"Nothing, Juni, just another woman asking if you were a Korean war orphan. Now go run inside and don't dawdle. Your father will be here soon."

I get my Samsonite suitcase that we got with Green Stamps out of my closet. I pack my PJs and my toothbrush and toothpaste and my green blankie and my silkie blankie and my pillow and my petkin bear. Then to the kitchen. Mommy doesn't like to bake so I bake all the cakes. For my birthday and for Daddy's birthday and for Christmas. For her birthday I bake lemon meringue pie with Eagle Brand. That's her favorite. The recipe for shortcake is on the Bisquick box. Milk, sugar, butter, and Bisquick in the bowl. I eat a little piece of butter. Salty melting.

"Can you manage, Juni, or is the dough too stiff? I'll give the dough a whack while you turn on the radio and make me a martini."

"With olive or onion?"

In a continuation of Communist aggression against India, the Chinese succeeded in capturing the Northeast Indian town of Tawang today ...

Preheat the oven to 425°. Then press out the dough and cut circles with a glass. Don't touch the dough too much or it will get tough. Circles onto the cookie sheet and into the oven. Once the gas caught the fat on fire and flames shot out of the oven and Mommy threw baking soda on it. So you always have to check and see if there's leftover fat in the broiler. Then I wash the red berries and pull out the green hull on top with the little metal gizmo from the market. Plp, plp, done. Plp, plp, done. Then slice them evenly. ¼ inch. Slice, slice, slice, done. Slice, slice, slice, done. Slice, slice. Eat. Perfumy, pinapply, flowerberry.

I pack the strawberries in one Tupperware, cooled off shortcakes in another, whipped cream spray can, paper picnic plates, and plastic spoons all together in a brown grocery bag. Ready to go. Daddy's here.

Mommy's stiff face. "(… Got everything you need? ... Who's handling your practice? – Nurse Sawada – Drive carefully ...) – Juni, put your things in the car. And Jay, be sure to call me and let me know when you're coming back."

We drive to the freeway.

"Welcome ladies and gentlemen to the Long Beach Freeway. We're at Signal Hill just off the Traffic Circle heading out PCH Pacific Coast Highway to the freeway. You'll see the freeway onramp coming up straight ahead. PCH onramp to the Long Beach Freeway, ladies and gentlemen, straight ahead."

"Uhhh, here's uhhh the pilot to the uhhh co-pilot."

"Co-pilot to pilot, Roger!" Smile.

"Uhhh, please advise uhhh next-uh freeway exit, uhhh, Roger."

"Roger, wilco! Next exit on the Long Beach Freeway is Willow Street exit, coming up Willow Street exit, Roger! Daddy, where're we really going?"

"Well, first up da Long Beach to da Santa Ana, then off inta da hills. How bout da mountains?

> The bear went over the mountain,
> The bear went over the mountain,
> The bear went over the mountain,
> To see what he could see.

How's dat?"

Daddy's voice makes my ears and the inside of the car vibrate.

"Come on, sing with me!

> And all that he could see,
> And all that he could see,
> Was the other side of the mountain,
> The other side of the mountain,
> The other side of the mountain,
> Was all that he could see.

It's gonna be a long trip, so why doncha grab that scrip in da back seat, help me learn my lines."

"Ok, but wait a minute." Out the window I look. Concrete and wires and cars. I try to think of nothing. Like Daddy on his *zafu*. Sitting on the *zafu* means thinking of nothing. I try. The silvery wing vent handle. Cross my eyes. Outside blurs by. Daddy once told Akiko and me about atoms. Everything is made of atoms. But they're so small you can't see them. Are there atoms in the wing vent handle? See between the atoms and think of nothing. Daddy drew a picture. Atoms with little things moving in circles around their center. Like in my book about the planets. The sun in the center, the planets around it. That is a solar system. Similar. Daddy's microscope makes things look big. If you put a big solar system under a humongous microscope can you see atoms? If you put the atoms under a microscope that was strong enough would you discover that the atom was really another solar system? Thinking something. Think nothing. Empty. I am in Los Angeles. Cars blurring. If atoms are so small and the solar system so large there must be so many atoms in the solar system you can't count them. If you can't count them then the people too. Are there more atoms in the solar system than people on earth? In the Milky Way? Is there another me? Uncountable atoms. Yes, there must be another person like me who looks exactly like me and does everything I do. Somewhere. How can I think of nothing?

Daddy's singing.

"We are climbing Jacob's Ladder
We are climbing Jacob's Ladder
We are climbing Jacob's Ladder
Brothers, Sisters, Ahh

Every rung goes higher, higher
Every rung goes higher, higher
Every rung goes higher, higher."

"Where are we now?"

"On the Ridge Route, issa long haul. Are ya gettin hungry? Get that *futomaki* granma made for us."

U Thant, Acting Secretary-General of the United Nations, met with representatives of the United States and Russia today in an effort to set up negotiations ...

It's dark and we finally eat strawberry shortcake. I spray whipped cream on top and add strawberries. Crusty outside, soft inside. Cake is crumbly and sweet and soft and berries are tart and juicy and cream is oily and thick. My fingers in Daddy's mouth. His tongue soft. Sticky. I close my eyes and open my mouth and spray whipped cream onto the strawberries in there. We drive through the black mountain night in our safe boat and the reading lamp lights the cake. We're full. It's dark outside and cold and the Cadillac's automatic headlight dimmer shifts the beams of light in front of us, long slots of light. A few trucks and us way out on our mysterious journey. Everything's gone. The night's a black velvet cape over us. Under Daddy's corduroy jacket is warm and has his smell. My head on his lap. Motor vibrating through his leg. I look up at Daddy. The gap between his two front teeth. Pull the jacket over my head.

> "Every rung goes higher, higher. Every rung goes higher, higher ..."

The morning sun hot through the windows. I wake up in the back seat of the car on my pillow and blankies. "Where are we, Daddy?"

"At a truck stop on the Grapevine. By Tejon Pass in the Tehachapis."

"I have to go *benjo*."

"Ok, allee-oop! There ya go. How bout if afterward we go visit Uncle Kenzo and Auntie Michiko in Fresno on the berry farm?"

On the Golden State Highway going up toward Bakersfield. Bugs on the windshield. It's hot and dry. Doesn't bother us. We have air conditioning.

"Sing me some songs, Juni. What about something from *West Side Story*?"

"Ok ... ok, guess who I am: I like to be in America."

"Hang on, what's the name of that character?"

"Cadillacs zoom in America."

"Oh, what's her name again, it's not Maria, it's ..."

"Life is all right in America, if you're all white in America. Can't you remember? It's Anita!"

"Thass right ... Rita Moreno played er in da movie ... Member when I took you and Akiko to da teater downtown to see da musical?"

"Yeah! And we sat up in the peanut gallery and watched with the beenoculars!"

"And you didn stop singin dose songs for months!"

"Ok, here's another one: What are we going to do about the other generation? How are we going to stop them when they start an explanation?"

"*Flower Drum Song!*"

"Yeah! We saw it last year. With Nancy Kwan ..."

"… and all those *Nisei* playing Chinese."

"Daddy, is it true what Akiko says that Japanese-Americans can't be in movies or on TV except for like Nancy Kwan in *Susie Wong*?"

"Well, Juni ... member da word I taught you d'other day, pre-juidice? Dat means, somebody pre-judges you. Dey already think a whachu can do or not, before ya do it. But Juni, remember: It's all in dare minds, that's all in d'other peoples' heads. Doesn't mean you can't do it. You can do whatever ya want, Juni."

"One more song, but this time I'm gonna try and trick you! *Two drifters, off to see the world.*"

"*Moon River ...*"

"*... and me.* Hey, Daddy! What's that over there?"

"Never seen it before, huh? Ts cottn."

We pull over. Sky powdery blue. Standing in the middle of the road in California. No one behind us, no one in front of us. Just miles of black asphalt and sandy earth and white, puffy cotton floating above it in the hot air. We walk over and play with the cotton plants and pick some. Thorny. Like mommy's roses. But you can do that. Just stop and pick it. And then we pull at the white puffy stuff coming out of the pods. The stuff sticks on something inside ... there are seeds. It's hard to get the cotton off.

"Yeah, that's hard work to remove the cotton from the seeds."

Funny. That's our clothes. My blouses are cotton. I take a pod with me and save it for a long, long time. Real cotton. From our trip.

"Ok, kiddo. Here we are!"

Berry farm. Old pick-up truck. Wooden shacks. Berry fields all over. Family running out to greet. "Hey, Uncle Juro's got a great new car! *Kombanwa* Juro, *kombanwa* Juni-chan. *Ehh, kawai-i, desne?* Cute little girl, isn't she. But those glasses! Hey, Juro, you're lucky – Uncle Tadao went fishing coupla days ago and caught a barracuda offa Santa Barbara. We still have some *sashimi*. Juni, you like *sashimi*?"

"Yeah, she loves the stuff, doncha, Juni?"

"And we have some *mochi* in the freezer left over from *Obon Festival*. We'll toast it and make dipping sauce with *shoyu* and sugar, ok, Juni-chan?"

Nod head.

Aunt Michiko cooks *skiyaki* for us. "Oh, Juni-chan can use *ohashi* now!"

"Gimme an egg, wudja, Michiko." Daddy cracks the egg in his bowl and whisks it with his *hashi*, swirls hot meat in it. Me too. It's gooshy. But salty and meaty.

"Here, Juni-chan, have some more *tofu* and vegetables."

After dinner I go play with the kids.

"Yeah, Juni, go run over there with them and make some poses like you always do so I can take some pictures."

"I have to go *benjo*."

"Hey kids, take Juni over to *benjo*, show her. She knows how outhouse works from her other cousins, but show her where the light and the paper is."

I don't like it. You have to walk way over in the field every time and squat when you pee.

"Ok, everybody, time for bed! Juni, you help your dad spread out the *futon*, there's room for both of you to sleep."

"Ok, kiddo, you had your glass of water. Need anything else? We're just out in the living room watching TV in case you do."

"Can we leave a little light on?"

"Yeah, sure, kiddo."

"Good night."

"G'night."

"Kenzo, I'm jus gonna go back and check ta make sure Juni's sleeping ok. Sometimes she gets homesick for her mom and can't fall asleep. Be right back ..."

Juni there ... asleep on the *futon* ... head on her small arm, light on her outstretched hand. Her nose, long lashes. A daughter. In my skin, but lighter. That's Azure. Her long hair. Not like mine bristly and black. Brown and soft, like Azure. Juni's activity. Inquisitiveness. Thirst for life. Listening and observing. To see the young mind, fresh, unstained. See it develop free. No constraints. No bowing and scraping. To see spirit. Try things out on her – myself, but separate. Uninhibited body. Not like me.

29

Live in a child's body again by watching it. Touching it. Stroking her hair. Her little arm ... arousal ... a young part of myself, part of my mind distinct from myself, dependent on me but independent. My body paired with another ... yet the child responds, understands as no partner can. Instinct. Small fingers touching me ... Juni finds childhood hidden in me. I continue my self in a new generation, my thought, my mind, my body – I survive through time ... being a parent ... love ... what is it? Too much ... afraid ...

"Juro, everything ok in there? How bout nother beer?"

"I'm coming ... jussa minute."

"Ohio, Juni-chan, good morning. Did you sleep well? Go run and get your father. There's news on the radio he should hear."

"He's on his *zafu.*"

"Well, get him anyway, it's important. Juro, geta load a this!"

We repeat this news just reaching us: In a surprise move last night, Moscow Radio announced Khrushchev's decision ordering Russian officers on Cuba to stop work on the rocket bases, crate the missiles, and ship them *home. But as U Thant prepares for his mission to Havana, Castro insists that the U.S. pull out of Guantanamo as a guarantee against future invasions ...*

"What's it mean, Daddy?"

"Means we cn drive home t'day. Gwon, start packin yr things. I'll call yr mom and you cn be in school on Monday."

"Hurry up, Juni, get a wiggle on! Get your things together, we have to leave in 15 minutes! Put on your best skirt and blouse. Did you brush your skirt? Remember what Connie says, brushing makes wool come alive! Did you floss? The principal is going to talk to you today."

"Hello, Mrs. Shimata. Hello, Juni."

"Hello, Mrs. Nielsen."

"Juni, we've decided we're going to put you in the fifth grade. This very day. You're going to skip the fourth grade how do you like that."

Eye blinks.

"So run over and get your things out of your desk in Mrs. Mader's room, and I'll bring you over to Mrs. Kayler's class."

"But I don't know *anyone* in the fifth grade!" Regina doesn't count.

"Don't worry, I'll introduce you, and you'll make friends quickly. Mrs. Kayler will help you. Now hurry along, get your things, we don't want to miss the bell for first period!"

On your back in the sandbox clouds move by. Funny feeling. No hurry. Floating. Like in water. Only dry. Bzzzzzz. The world is round. I live on the round world. Way over there kids playing. Sky blue. No time. Only clouds floating up there, moving past.

In my tummy. Out.

In. Out.

Explanatory notes and Q&A for this text can be found at the website http://www.junishimata.com/blog/ under the tag *Road Girl*.

If you enjoyed *Road Girl*, I would appreciate your honest evaluation in the form of a review on Amazon or Goodreads.com. Thank you! Vanessa

Vanessa Araya

ROAD GIRL

Eine Erzählung

MAMA WEINEND neben dem Radio in der Küche. Mama weint nie. „Mama! Was ist los!"

Los Angeles, 17:15 Uhr. Sie hatte am Samstag ihren Psychiater, Dr. Ralph Greenson, angerufen und sich über Schlaflosigkeit beklagt. Er habe ihr geraten, eine Spazierfahrt zu machen, berichtete die Polizei.

Manchmal erzählt Mama die Geschichte wie ihr Papi starb und danach ihre Mama. Manchmal weint sie.

Dr. Greenson hat einen Schürhaken vom Kamin geholt, ein Fenster eingeschlagen und das Zimmer betreten. Er sagte Kommissar R. E. Byron, dass Frau Monroe bis über die Schultern von einem Laken und einer champagnerfarbenen Decke zugedeckt war.

„Ich weiß es nicht, Engelchen. Ich fühle mich so t-traurig ... so a-allein."

So viele Tränen! Mama hat blonde Haare vorne. Heißt Wasserstoff. Blonde Locken wie eine gehörnte Muschel da über ihr nasses Gesicht.

„Es wird schon gut, mein Herz." Sie putzt sich die Nase. „Zurück an die Arbeit! Wie haben keine Zeit zu vergeuden. Hast du deine Wollröcke von der Aussteuertruhe geholt?"

Aus-steuer-tru-he. Der Holzkasten von daheim, der so streng riecht. Tötet die Motten. „Heute ist zu heiß für Wollröcke!"

„Kopf hoch. Ich lege eine Platte auf. Wie wäre es mit Brubecks *Take Five...*"

So heiß. Besser im schattigen Schlafzimmer wo die Jalousette immer geschlossen bleibt. Oder auf dem Fliesenboden im Badezimmer. Silberfischchen in den Ecken. Bald fängt die Schule wieder an.

„Komm schon, Altkleidersammlung der Heilsarmee nächste Woche und am Wochenende danach eine Einkaufstour in Bevrlyills mit Connie also sortier deine alten Röcke aus um Platz zu machen. Dalli! Die Babysitterin kommt in drei Stunden und ich muss noch meine Haare machen!"

„Näht Connie diesmal etwas für *mich*?"

„Das habe ich dir schon erklärt. Du bist zu jung und du wächst zu schnell. Es ... lohnt sich nicht, in Kleider für dich zu investieren da du so schnell herauswächst, aber sie wird die Farben ko-ordinieren und die Falten in deinen Röcken verstärken damit sie besser hängen."

Besser hängen? „Mama, das Telefon."

„Geh mal ran, es könnte dein Vater sein. Ich muss mit ihm reden. Hallo, Jay? Juni, geh in dein Zimmer, während ich mit deinem Vater spreche."

Bei Patience legt man eine Figur auf, dann legt man drei Karten um. Drei Karten um. Schwarz geht auf Rot. Rot geht auf Schwarz. Reihen baut man auf Assen. Ein König kommt auf einen leeren Platz. Wenn alle Karten abgelegt sind, ist die Patience aufgegangen. Manchmal geht's ohne Schummeln, aber eigentlich nie.

Und das, liebe Zuhörer, war unser Samstagsvormittags-programm hier auf KPFK, dem freien Pacifica-Runkfunk in Los Angeles – gesendet mit 75.000 Watt von Mount Wilson – mit Werken von Mozart, Beethoven und Brahms.

Mama bewegt ihr Bein über das Pedal. Es heißt Kupplung. „Connie, habe ich dir erzählt, dass die Mädels vom Büro einen Ausflug nach Las Vegas für den Herbst planen?"

„Mmmm mmmm, ja, meine Liebe. Brauchst du dafür neue Kleider? Ich habe einige sehr kurzen Röcke gesehen diese Saison, ich glaube, man nennt sie Miniröcke."

„Bei *meinen* Knien?"

„Nun, wie wäre es mit Hosen, du bist ja so groß ... weißt du, Courrèges hat Balenciaga verlassen und seinen eigenen Modesalon mit einem Hosenanzug diesen Herbst eröffnet. Ich habe wunderschöne türkisen Bouretteseiden-Muster dabei, die Farbe unterstreicht deine Augen – wir könnten einen Stoff bei Magnins suchen."

Die Haare von alter Connie fallen runter und sie steckt sie wieder hoch. Sie ist dick und hat Körpergeruch. Kupplung, Gas geben, Schau-in-den-Spiegel. Der schlechte Auto Geruch. Wie Tankstellen. „Wie lange noch bis wir da sind? Mir ist schlecht."

Und jetzt Musik von den Salzburger Festspielen: Verdis *Requiem* mit Hu-bert van Kray-jan und die Berliner Philharmoniker.

„Der Long Beach Freeway. Long Beach Boulevard, Ausfahrt rechts. Meine Damen und Herren, Compton Boulevard, Ausfahrt 2 Meilen rechts. Bitte links einordnen, Ausfahrt rechts. Imperial Highway, Ausfahrt in 4½ Meilen. Bitte links einordnen ... „

„Juni, hör auf mit dem Quatsch!"

„Wieso? Ich bin Radiomoderator und kündige die Ausfahrten an."

„Sei still! Ich muss mich aufs Fahren konzentrieren."

„Balenciagas Kostüm steht dir, aber du hast sein Sack-Kleid nicht gemocht," sagt Connie. „Der taillierte Chanel-Look passt besser zu dir. Und habe ich's dir erzählt, *Vogue* hat einen neuen Herausgeber – eine Frau."

„Ich überleg mir, ein neues Auto zu kaufen. Ich habe diesen alten Ford, seitdem wir in das Haus vor sieben Jahren eingezogen sind."

Die Vorderzähne von Connie sind pelzig und rot vom Lippenstift. Sie bewegt die Zunge drüber und schmatzt. „Aber die Farb' von deinem Auto ist so nett, so, mit dem roten Dach und der Rest grau und so ..."

„Ach, dieser alte Mainline. Es gibt ein neues Modell – Falcon. Hast vielleicht die Werbung gsehen, eventuell kauft es Junis Vater für uns."

„Der Hollywood Freeway. Bitte einordnen, meine Damen und Herren, nach rechts. Die beiden Spuren rechts Ausfahrt zum Hollywood Freeway ..."

„Juni, was habe ich gesagt! Muss ich hier anhalten und bis drei zählen? Und was ist mit deinem Sicherheitsgurt – warum bist du nicht angeschnallt? Wie oft muss ich dir das sagen!"

Connie schaut gerade aus auf den Freeway.

„Aber es tut meinem Bauch weh. Ich habe *Bauchweh*!"

„Azure, wir fahren zuerst nach Bullocks, nicht wahr?"

„Ja, Connie, das hier ist Wilshire Boulevard."

Ein Farbiger in Uniform kommt das Auto zu parken. Mama sagt, dass Farbige sind wie Weiße, aber sie riechen anders.

„Behalten Sie das Kleingeld."

„Meine Güte, Juni, das Labor-Day-Wochenende ist fast schon vorbei, und die Schule fängt am Dienstag an! Sind all deine Blusen gebügelt? Du kannst spät aufbleiben und *Bonanza* anschauen."

Wir haben ein neues Bügelbrett das vir-stell-bar ist. Man kann es niedriger stellen. Mit meiner Brille kann ich TV gucken wenn ich bügele. Little Joe ist der Beste, Hoss ist seltsam. Man gibt destilliertes Wasser in das Bügeleisen, stellt es auf Baumwolle und drückt den Dampfknopf. Zuerst macht man den Kragen, Rückseite, dann Vorderseite. Blusen-Bügel-Geruch. Süß. Seifig. Toast. Wolle bügeln riecht nach Kaka. Manchmal wenn Mama bügelt lässt sie einen Fuf fahren und kichert. Sie sagt, Fuf ist kurz für Fu-fu auf Japanisch, aber sie ist weiß. Daddy ist japanisch und er nennt es Fart. Dann bügelt man die Schulter, Manschetten und Ärmel. Zuletzt den Körper. So knittert die Bluse beim Bügeln nicht. „Ich habe die rosa Bluse und die kurzärmelige geschafft."

„Nun, mach auch die langärmelige und die hellblaue, dann hast du für die ganze Woche. Und morgen kannst du die Schuhe putzen."

„Schnell, Juni!" Hast du das Gesicht gewaschen und die Zähne geputzt? Hast du deine Butterbrotdose und deine Thermosflasche mit Milch? Komm, beeil dich, du willst nicht am ersten Schultag zu spät sein! Steig auf die Rückbank ein und schnall dich an. Kein Rumwursteln damit, meine Dame! Ich gehe mit dir heute rein, ich muss mit deiner Lehrerin reden. Da, lauf mal rüber und bring deine Brotzeitdose weg. Guten Tag, Frau Mader. Ich bin Junis Mutter, Frau Shimata."

„... sprachbegabt ... immer Fragen ... zu weit voraus ..."

In der vierten Klasse man geht zu Frau Mader in ein anderes Gebäude. Frau Mader hat Fältchen und ist weich und rund. Puderig. Blasse rote Haare. Man kann ihre Kopfhaut sehen. Zimmer mit niedriger Decke. Stickig. Aus dem Fenster der heiße Asphaltspielplatz und der Sandkasten. Blauer Himmel und Wolken. Bei Frau Mader haben wir ein großes Erdkundebuch und wir lesen über Ägypten und der Sinai. Sie sagt, der Prinz von England so alt ist wie wir. Vielleicht können wir ihn heiraten, wenn wir hübsch sind. Wir lernen ein paar Worte auf Spanisch. *Quiero comer. ¿Que hora es?* Jeden Tag nach der Schule bleibe ich bis Mama kommt mich abholen. Manchmal wird es dunkel. Wir spielen Bomben über Tokio. Ich bin Tokio. Die anderen werfen Bomben. Es dauert lange nach Hause zu fahren. Es gibt Stau und Mama benutzt die Kupplung. Mir wird schlecht.

„Denk nicht dran, Juni, es geht vorbei. Hör einfach Radio."

Unsere Führerschaft in Wissenschaft und Industrie, unsere Hoffnung für Frieden und Sicherheit, unsere Verpflichtung uns selbst gegenüber, aber auch anderen – das alles verlangt, dass wir uns anstrengen, diese Rätsel zu lösen – für das Wohl der Menschheit die führende Weltraumfahrtnation zu werden.

„Hast du gehört, was Präsident Kennedy sagt, Juni? Wir sind in einem Wettlauf ins All mit Russland, und wir wollen gewinnen. Du könntest helfen. Möchtest du Russische lernen?"

Regina ist zurückgeblieben. Regina ist ein komischer Name. Klingt wie Vagina. Sie ist in der fünften Klasse aber sie ist vierzehn Jahre alt. Sie ist größer als alle anderen und sie bekommt ihre Tage. Sie hat immer eine Spezialtasche mit Zeug. Sie lässt sie bei der Garderobe. Manchmal riecht sie nach

Fisch. Ihre Brille macht ihre Augen groß. Rosarotes Gestell hoch in den Ecken mit kleinen Glitzersteinchen. Regina half mir an meinem ersten Schultag. Mama erzählt mir immer davon. Mama war früher So-zi-all-arbeiterin. Sie hat Fälle bearbeitet. Manchmal bin ich mit ihr zu den Fällen gefahren. Sie hielt ihre Ordner fest und hat den Farbigen zugelächelt und ihre Zähne gezeigt und nach unten geschaut und genickt mit dem Kopf. Jetzt ist sie Sekretärin bei Raytheon und sie steht gerade und zieht den Po ein. Regina trägt immer den gleichen roten Rock. Nicht schön. Die Falten hängen nicht richtig. Sie ist seltsam. Ich spreche nicht mehr mit ihr. Einmal hat Joe Bell Scheiße gesagt und Herr Kirch hat ihm Borax-Seife aus der Toilette in den Mund geschmiert und Joe ist rumgerannt 20 Minuten lang mit seinem Mund weit aufgerissen und er hatte große Augen und Angst. Aber wir haben gehört wie auch Herr Kirch geflucht hat. Einmal im Schatten auf dem Asphalt Larry und ich sagten uns wir würden einander unsers zeigen also zeigte ich Larry meins wie bei Daddy aber Larry hat mir nicht seins gezeigt und Herr Kirch hat uns entdeckt. Na und? Mama war es egal aber Herr Kirch tat mir weh.

„Jedenfalls, Juni, ich habe mit deinem Vater gesprochen und du musst nicht mehr die Wochenenden bei ihm verbringen. Er kommt mittwochs und holt dich nach der Schule ab, hörst du? Er parkt vor der Schule und wartet auf dich. Okay?"

EEY 115

Da ist sein silberner Cadillac.

Der hat die größten Heckflossen von allen. Auf der Seite steht Sixty Special in Kursivschrift, wie wir letztes Jahr in Schönschreiben gelernt haben und hinten steht Fleetwood in Druckbuchstaben. Er hat eine besonders gemachte Kopfstütze denn Daddy hat ein Schleuder Trauma und muss einen Halsschaal immer tragen. Einmal hat Kusine Akiko ihre Periode gekriegt auf dem Rücksitz und nichts gesagt und Blut war auf dem grauen Polster das kann man noch sehen und Daddy hat einen nassen Schwamm eine Woche lang draufgelegt und hat es immer gerieben und sagte Dummes Mädchen. Aber meistens mag er ihre Tittis. Mama sagt Brüste oder Oberteil aber wir sagen Tittis. Daddys Auto ist durcheinander und voll mit Zeug. Wie sein Haus. Viele Gummis, Zahnseide überall, da wir sie jeden Tag verwenden müssen, die Pistole mit dem weißen Griff, die *zafu* die Omi für ihn gemacht hat für wenn er meditiert, sein Stethoskop und Fernrohr und Bongos, Orangen denn Daddy hat mir von seinem Traum erzählt – er

44

hat ein Serum aus Orangen hergestellt und Opas Leben gerettet denn er musste Orangen ernten als Bub auf der Farm in Riverside – die Exakta und die Asahi Pentax und die braune Leder Kamerakiste und viele Rollfilme überall und viele Stifte und Papier und Skizzenhefte und Theaterstücke und Texte zu lernen. Und seine braune Cordjacke. Ich darf die Pistole nicht berühren aber die Gummis schon. Sie riechen wie alles aus Gummi wie der Ball in der Schule. Es gibt die kleinen in der flachen Verpackung wie Kaugummi wo Trojan-Enz drauf steht und die in den kleinen blauen Plastikdöschen mit japanischen Buchstaben drauf. Ich rolle sie aus und blase sie auf und dann habe ich Gummi und Talkum auf den Lippen. Und ich muss Rollen mit ihm üben. Ich muss die Rollen spielen wie letztes Jahr, als ich jeden Abend auf der Bühne in der Morgan Hall auf Locust Street bei der Schule stand und ich hatte einen dunkelroten Samtmantel und eine Krone und ich hatte ein Zepter und Joe Bell, der früher in der Besserungsanstalt war, hat vor mir einen Steptanz gemacht und man konnte mein Lied nicht hören denn er war so laut und Daddy hat eine Million Fotos geknipst.

Aus dem Cadillac Musik.

Wir fahren fort mit der Hitparade dieser Woche, aber zuerst ein Blick zurück auf den Nummer-Eins-Hit des letzten Monats von Neil Sedaka!

Doo-doo-doo
Down doobie-doo down-down, kamma kamma
Girl there's just no livin'
With-ou-ou-out you ...

Der Fahrer betrachtet Juni.

Da ist sie, mein Juni-chan. Neue Brille. Gläser so dick wie meine, armes Kind. Sie wird groß. Muss ihr einiges beibringen ...

... Don't take you-ur love away from me
Re-mem-ber whe-en you held me tight
And you kissed me all throoooough the night

"Hallo, Kleine, wie steht's? Willst keine Wochenenden mehr mit mir verbringen, oder wie? Was soll's, gib uns 'nen Kuss. Was hast heute in der Schule g'macht?"

"Frau Mader und Erdkunde."

„Ich möchte dir auch 'n paar Dinge beibringen heut, okay?"

Augenrollen.

„Guck mal her ... wo's mein Skizzbuch ... Dies hier is'n Mann, okay? Und du weiß', er hat 'nen Penis."

Schon wieder.

„Und er hat diese kleinen Dinger die schwimmen, die heißen Spermien, weißte? Und dies hier is'ne Frau. Sie hat ein Ei, eine Ei-zelle."

Na und?

„Wenn der Sperma trifft die Eizelle, es heißt Be-fruch-tung, und die Eizelle fängt an sich zu teilen, so:

Zuerst in zwei, dann in vier, und so weiter. Verstehst? Bis alle Zellen eines Babys da sind, wie Baby Juni."

„Daddy, wo gehen wir heute Abend essen?"

„Na komm, das hier is' wichtig, pass auf. Und bevor sie eine Eizelle produziere kann, muss sie die Menstruation haben."

„Ja, aber ich habe Hun - ger."

„Haste verstanden?"

„Der Mann hat 'nen Penis und die Spermas und die Dame hat das Ei und sie muss men-iju-strie-ren und dann teilt sich das Ei und macht das Baby."

„Men-stru-ier-en. Also dann. Wenn du willst können wir zur Bucht fahren, ich schwimm und dann können wir Fischstäbchen essen."

„Mit Remoulade?"

„Ja."

„O ja Fischstäbchen! Fahren wir!"

Und jetzt beenden wir unseren Top-Ten-Countdown mit dem Nummer-Eins-Hit von den Four Seasons!

Sher-er-rry, Sherry baby
I'm gonna make-a you mi-yi-yi-ine

Juni und ihre Mutter sind im Ford auf dem Heimweg von der Schule.

In dieser Angelegenheit haben auch vor der U.S. Botschaft in Prag mehr als 1.000 Tschechoslowaken gegen die amerikanische Seeblockade von Kuba demonstriert. ,Yankees raus' haben sie skandiert.

„Mir ist übel."

„Denk an was anderes, Juni. Dein Vater kommt heute Abend. Es sind schon zwei Wochen seit seinem letzten Besuch und er holt dich nachher ab."

„Heute Abend? Wieso? Weil er gestern nicht gekommen ist?"

„Nein, er nimmt dich auf eine Reise mit."

„Aber morgen ist Freitag. Wenn er mich jetzt mitnimmt verpasse ich die Schule. Außerdem hast du gesagt ich muss keine Wochenenden mehr bei ihm verbringen."

„Diesmal ist anders. Du sollst deine Sachen packen. Du bleibst einige Tage fort."

„Wo fahren wir hin? Muss ich Spritzen bekommen, wie als er nach Japan geflogen ist? Wenn ich Spritzen bekomme gehe ich nicht mit!"

„Keine Spritzen, beruhige dich. Vielleicht fahrt ihr zusammen in die Wüste. Es wird eine Überraschung."

„Warum muss immer alles mit Daddy eine Überraschung sein? Darf ich beim Ballett fehlen?"

„Ja."

„Yipiieh!" Ich hasse Ballett. Die alte Lebedeff stupst mich immer mit dem Stock in den Po.

„Du hast deinen Vater seit seinem Geburtstag nicht mehr gesehen. Du kannst einen Kuchen für ihn backen, wenn du schnell machst."

„Erdbeerkuchen?"

„Wenn du willst. Schau, wir sind gerade beim McDaniels-Markt. Lauf schnell und hol eine Dose Sprühsahne und ich hole die Erdbeeren. Wir treffen uns an der Kasse in Nullkommanichts …"

„… Nein, ist sie nicht! Ich habe sie selbst gebärt!"

„Mama, was ist?"

„Nichts, Juni, nur wieder eine Frau die fragt, ob du eine koreanische Kriegswaise bist. Jetzt lauf schnell ins Haus und trödle nicht. Bald kommt dein Vater."

Vom Schrank hole ich meinen Samsonite-Koffer die wir mit den grünen Treuemarken gekriegt haben.

Ich packe mein Pyjama und meine Zahnbürste und Zahnpaste und meine grüne Decki und meine Seide-Decki und mein Kissen und mein Steiff-Bären. Dann in die Küche. Mama mag nicht backen, also backe ich immer die Kuchen. Für meinen Geburtstag und für Daddys und für Weihnachten. Für Mamas Geburtstag backe ich Zitronen-Meringue-Torte mit gesüßter Kondensmilch. Ihr Favorit. Das Rezept für Erdbeerkuchen steht auf der Bisquick-Packung. Milch, Zucker, Butter und Bisquick in die Schüssel. Ein kleines Stückchen Butter für mich. Salzig schmelzend.

„Geht das, Juni, oder ist der Teig zu steif? Ich schlag mal den Teig während du das Radio anmachst und mir ein Martini mixt."

„Mit Olive oder Silberzwiebel?"

In einer Fortsetzung kommunistischer Aggressionen gegen Indien ist es der Volksrepublik China heute gelungen, die nordindischen Stadt Tawang einzunehmen ...

Den Herd auf 220 Grad vorheizen. Dann den Teig flach drücken und Kreise mit einem Glas ausschneiden. Den Teig nicht zu viel berühren, sonst wird er zäh. Die Kreise auf das Kuchenblech legen und in den Backofen. Einmal hat das Fett unterm Gas Feuer gefangen und Flammen schossen raus aus dem Herd und Mama hat Backnatron drauf geworfen. Deswegen muss man immer vorher schauen ob übrig gebliebenes Fett unterm Salamander ist. Dann wasche ich die roten Beeren und zupfe die grünen Blätter oben drauf mit dem kleinen Metalldingsbums von McDaniels. Zp, zp, fertig. Zp, zp, fertig. Dann schneiden. Immer einen halben Zentimeter dick. Schnitt, schnitt, schnitt, fertig. Schnitt, schnitt, schnitt, fertig. Schnitt, schnitt. Mmmm. Parfümig, annanassig, Blumenbeere.

Ich packe die Erdbeeren in eine Tupperdose, abgekühlte Kuchen in eine andere, Schlagsahne-Dose, Picknick-Pappteller und Plastiklöffel alle zusammen in eine braune Einkaufstüte. Alles fertig. Daddy ist da.

Mamas saures Gesicht. „(… Hast alles was du brauchst? … Wer übernimmt die Praxis? – Krankenschwester Sawada – Fahr vorsichtig …) – Juni, bring deine Sachen ins Auto. Und Jay, ruf mich an und lass mich wissen, wann ihr zurückkommt."

Wir fahren zum Freeway.

„Willkommen meine Damen und Herren zum Long Beach Freeway. Wir befinden uns gerade auf Signal Hill neben dem Traffic Circle und fahren in Richtung PCH Pacific Coast Highway zum Freeway. Gerade aus sehen Sie die Auffahrt. PCH-Auffahrt zum Long

Beach Freeway, meine Damen und Herren, gerade aus."

„Ähhh – Pilot zum – ähh – Ko-Pilot."

„Ko-Pilot zum Pilot, verstanden!" Lächeln.

„Ähhh, – bitte um Auskunft – ähhh – nächste Ausfahrt, kommen."

„Wird ausgeführt. Nächste Ausfahrt aus dem Long Beach Freeway ist Willow Street Ausfahrt, nächste Ausfahrt, Willow Street, kommen! Daddy, wo fahren wir wirklich hin?"

„Nun, zuerst die Long Beach bis zum Santa Ana Freeway, danach bis zur Anhöhe. Wie wär's mit den Bergen?

The bear went over the mountain,
The bear went over the mountain,
The bear went over the mountain,
To see what he could see.

Na?"

Daddys Stimme vibriert das ganze Auto, auch meine Ohren.

„Komm, sing mit!

And all that he could see,
And all that he could see,
Was the other side of the mountain,
The other side of the mountain,
The other side of the mountain,
Was all that he could see.

Es wird eine lange Fahrt, Kleine. Hol mal das Drehbuch von dr Rücksitz, hilf mir meinen Text zu lernen."

„Okay, aber warte." Ich schau aus dem Fenster. Beton und Telefonleitungen und Autos. Ich versuch an nichts zu denken. Wie Daddy auf seinem *zafu*. Auf dem *zafu* sitzen bedeutet an nichts denken. Ich versuch's. Der silberne Flügelfenstergriff. Augen kreuzen. Draußen unscharf. Einmal erzählte Daddy Akiko und mir von den Atomen. Alles besteht aus Atomen. Aber sie sind so winzig man kann sie nicht sehen. Gibt es Atome im Flügelfenstergriff? Zwischen den Atomen gucken und an nichts denken. Daddy hatte ein Bild skizziert. Atome mit kleinen Dingern um sie in Kreisen drehend. Wie in meinem Buch über die Planeten. Die Sonne in der Mitte, die Planeten rund herum. Das ist ein Solarsystem. Ähnlich. Daddys Mikroskop macht Sachen groß. Wenn du ein großes Solarsystem unter ein riesiges Mikroskop stellen könntest, entdeckst du dass ein Atom eigentlich ein anderes Solarsystem ist? Etwas denken. Nichts denken. Leer. Ich bin in Los Angeles. Autos zoomen vorbei. Wenn die Atome so klein sind und das Solarsystem so groß dann gibt es so viele Atome im Solarsystem du kannst sie nicht alle zählen. Wenn nicht, dann auch die Menschen nicht. Gibt es mehr Atome im Solarsystem als Menschen auf der Erde? In der Milchstraße? Gibt es mich noch einmal?

Unzählige Atome. Ja, es muss mich nochmals geben die genauso aussieht wie ich und alles tut was ich tue. Irgendwo. Wie kann ich an nichts denken?

Daddy singt.

„We are climbing Jacob's Ladder
We are climbing Jacob's Ladder
We are climbing Jacob's Ladder
Brothers, Sisters, Ahh

Every rung goes higher, higher
Every rung goes higher, higher
Every rung goes higher, higher."

„Wo sind wir jetzt?"

„Auf der Ridge Route, 's ist 'ne lange Strecke. Hast Hunger? Hol das *futomaki* die Oma gmacht hat."

U Thant, amtierender UN-Generalsekretär, hat sich heute mit Vertretern der USA und Russlands getroffen und versucht, einen Verhandlungstermin zu vereinbaren ...

Es ist dunkel und endlich essen wir den Erdbeerkuchen. Ich sprühe Sahne drauf und lege die Beeren dazu. Draußen krustig, innen weich. Cake ist krümelig und süß und weich und Beeren sind säuerlich und saftig und Sahne ist ölig und dick. Meine Finger in Daddys Mund. Seine Zunge weich. Klebrig. Ich schließe die Augen und öffne meinen Mund und sprühe Sahne auf die Erdbeeren drinnen. Wir fahren durch die schwarze Bergnacht in unserem sicheren Boot und die Leselampe beleuchtet den Kuchen. Wir sind satt. Es ist dunkel draußen und kalt und das Abblendlicht vom Cadillac ist automatisch und wechselt Lichtspuren vor uns, lange Lichtschachten. Ein paar LKWs und wir weit draußen auf unserer geheimen Fahrt. Alles ist weg. Die Nacht ein schwarzer Samtmantel über uns. Unter Daddys Cordjacke ist warm. Riecht nach ihm. Mein Kopf auf seinem Schoß. Der Motor vibriert durch sein Bein. Ich schaue hinauf zu Daddy. Die Lücke zwischen seinen Vorderzähnen. Ziehe die Jacke über meinen Kopf.

„Every rung goes higher, higher. Every rung goes higher, higher ...“

Die Morgensonne ist heiß durch die Fenster. Auf der Rückbank werde ich wach mit meinem Kissen und meinen Decken. „Wo sind wir, Daddy?“

„'ne Raststätte auf der Grapevine. Bei Tejon-Pass in den Tehachapi-Bergen.“

„Ich muss *benjo*.“

„Okay, allee-oop! Da. Wie wär's wenn wir nachher Onkel Kenzo und Tante Michiko in Fresno auf der Beeren-Farm besuchen?“

Auf der Golden State Highway Richtung Bakersfield. Fliegen auf der Windschutzscheibe. Es ist heiß und trocken. Stört uns nicht. Wir haben Klimaanlage.

„Sing mir 'n paar Lieder, Juni. Etwas aus *West Side Story*?"

„Okay ... okay, rate mal wer ich bin: I like to be in America."

„Warte mal, wie heißt die Figur noch?"

„Cadillacs zoom in America."

„Wie heißt sie noch einmal, es ist nicht die Maria, es ist, es ist ..."

„Life is all right in America, if you're all white in America. Kannst du dich nicht erinnern? Es ist Anita!"

„Jaaa, richtig. Rita Moreno im Film, gell? Kannst dich erinnern als ich dich und Akiko zum Musical im Theater Downtown genommen habe?"

„Ja! Und wir saßen auf der höchsten Galerie und haben mit dem Fernglas geguckt!"

„Und du hast die Lieder noch Monate lang gesungen!"

„Okay, hier ist noch ein Lied zum Raten: What are we going to do about the other generation? How are we going to stop them when they start an explanation?"

„*Flower Drum Song!*"

"Ja! Wir haben's letztes Jahr im Kino gesehen, mit Nancy Kwan ..."

„… und mit all den *Nisei* die Chinesen gespielt haben.“

„Daddy, stimmt es, was Akiko sagt, dass Japano-Amerikaner nicht im Kino spielen können oder im Fernsehen außer wie Nancy Kwan in *Susie Wong*?“

„Also, Juni … kannst dich an das Wort erinnern, das ich vor 'n paar Tag' gsagt hab: Vor-ur-teil? Bedeutet jemand urteilt dich vorab. Er weiß was du machen kannst und was nicht, bevor du was getan hast. Aber denk dran, Juni: Das ist nur in den Köpfen. In den Köpfen anderer Leute. Bedeutet nicht, dass du es nicht kannst. Du kannst alles machen, was du willst, Juni.“

„Noch ein Lied, Daddy. Aber jetzt leg ich dich rein: Two drifters, off to see the world.“

„Moon River …“

„… and me. Hey, Daddy! Was ist das drüben?“

„Hast nie gsehen? Baumwoll.“

Wir halten an. Himmel taubenblau. Stehen mitten auf dem Highway in Kalifornien. Niemand hinter uns. Niemand vor uns. Nur meilenweit schwarzer Asphalt und sandige Erde und weiße, flauschige Baumwolle drüber in der heißen Luft. Wir gehen rüber zu den Baumwollpflanzen und pflücken. Dornig, wie Mamas Rosen. Aber man darf das. Einfach anhalten und pflücken. Dann ziehen wir an der weißen Watte die aus den Kapseln kommt. Das

Zeug klebt auf was drinnen ... es gibt Samen. Schwer die Baumwolle von den Samen zu trennen.

„Siehst du, Baumwolle von den Samen zu trennen ist schwere Arbeit."

Komisch. Das sind unsere Kleider. Meine Blusen sind aus Baumwolle. Ich nehm eine Kapsel mit und hebe sie für eine lange, lange Zeit auf. Echte Baumwolle. Von unsrer Reise.

„Okay, Kleine. Wir sind da!"

Beeren-Farm. Alter kleiner Laster. Holzhütten. Erdbeerfelder überall. Familie rennt zu uns. „Hey, Onkel Juro hat ein tolles neues Auto! *Kombanwa* Juro, *kombanwa* Juni-chan. *Ehh, kawai-i, desne?* Hübsches Mädel ist das. Aber die Brille! Hey, Juro, ihr habt Glück – Onkel Tadao war vor ein paar Tagen angeln und hat eine Barrakuda bei Santa Barbara gfangen. Wir haben noch etwas *sashimi* übrig. Juni, magst du *sashimi?*"

„Ja, sie liebt das Zeug. Gell, Juni?"

„Und es gibt noch *mochi* in der Gefriertruhe vom *Obon-Fest.* Wir rösten es und machen einen Dip mit *shoyu* und Zucker, okay, Juni-chan?"

Kopf nicken.

Tante Michiko kocht *skiyaki* für uns.

„Ähh, Juni-chan kann inzwischen *hashi* benutzen!"

„Gib mir'n Ei, Michiko." Daddy schlägt das Ei in seine Schale und quirlt es mit seinen *hashi*, tunkt dann das heiße Fleisch drin. Ich auch. Es ist schlupfig. Aber salzig und fleischig.

„Nimm, Juni-chan, mehr *tofu* und Gemüse."

Nach dem Abendessen gehe ich mit den anderen Kindern spielen.

„Ja, renn mal, Juni, drüben. Spiel' mal schön zusammen und macht einige Posen, wie immer für mich, damit ich Fotos knipsen kann.

„Ich muss *benjo*."

„Oh - kay. Hey, Mädels, nimm Juni mit zum *benjo*, zeig's ihr. Sie kennt schon das Plumpsklo von anderen Kusinen, aber zeig' ihr wo's Papier is'."

Ich mag's nicht. Es ist dunkel und man muss in der Hocke Pipi machen und jedes Mal weit weg ins Feld hinlaufen.

„Hört alle her, Kinder, Zeit ins Bett zu gehen! Juni, hilf deinem Vater den *futon* auszubreiten, da könnt ihr zusammen schlafen."

„Okay, Kleine, du hast dein Glas Wasser gehabt. Brauchst noch was? Wir sind draußen und schauen fern, falls du was brauchst."

„Können wir das kleine Licht an lassen?"

„Aber klar doch."

„Gute Nacht."

„G' Nacht."

„Kenzo, ich schau mal kurz zu Juni, ob sie ruhig schläft. Manchmal hat sie Heimweh nach ihrer Mutter und kann nicht einschlafen. Bin gleich wieder da ...“

Juni da ... schläft auf dem *futon* ... Kopf auf dem kleinen Arm, Licht fällt auf der Hand. Ihre Nase, lange Wimpern. Eine Tochter. In meiner Haut, aber heller. Das ist Azure. Ihr langes Haar. Nicht borstig und schwarz wie meine. Braun und weich, wie Azure. So quirlig und wissbegierig. Durst nach Leben. Sie horcht und beobachtet. Den jungen Verstand erleben, frisch, unbelastet. Zusehen wie er sich frei entfaltet. Ohne Zwang. Ohne Katzbuckeln. Geist sehen. Sachen an ihm ausprobieren – an mir selbst, aber getrennt. Unverkrampfter Körper. Nicht wie ich. Wieder im Kinderkörper leben können durch Beobachten. Berühren. Ihre Haare streicheln. Ihr kleiner Arm ... Erregung ... ein junger Teil von mir selbst, Teil meines Verstandes, aber verschieden, abhängig von mir aber unabhängig. Mein Körper gepaart mit einem anderen ... aber das Kind reagiert, versteht, wie kein Partner kann. Instinkt. Kleine Finger, die mich berühren ... Juni findet die verschwundene Kindheit in mir. Ich dauere fort in einer neuen Generation – meine Gedanken, mein

Geist, mein Körper – überleben durch die Zeit ...
Eltern sein ... Liebe ... was ist das? Ist zu viel ...
Angst ...

„Juro, alles okay bei euch? Willst noch 'n Bier?"

„Ja, ich komme ... Augenblick."

„*Ohio,* Juni-chan, guten Morgen. Hast du gut
geschlafen? Lauf schnell und hol' deinen Vater. Es
gibt Nachrichten im Radio."

„Er sitzt auf seinem *zafu.*"

„Hol' ihn trotzdem, es ist wichtig. Juro! Hör mal
her!"

Wir wiederholen die Nachricht, die uns soeben erreicht
hat: In einer überraschenden Wende gestern Abend hat
Radio Moskau Chruschtschows Befehl bekanntgegeben,
ab sofort die Arbeit an den Raketen-Basen auf Kuba zu
stoppen. Die Raketen werden zusammengepackt und
nach Hause geschickt. Aber während U Thant
Vorbereitungen für seine Mission nach Havanna trifft,
pocht Castro darauf, dass die USA sich aus Guantanamo
zurückziehen, als Garant gegen künftige Invasionen.

„Was bedeutet das, Daddy?"

„Bedeutet, dass wir heut' nach Haus fahren können. Geh, pack deine Sachen zammen. Ich ruf' deine Mutter an und Montag bist in der Schule."

EEV 115

„Beeil dich, Juni, beweg deinen Hintern! Hol deine Sachen, wir müssen in 15 Minuten aus dem Haus! Zieh deinen besten Rock und deine beste Bluse an. Hast du den Rock gebürstet? Du weißt wie Connie immer sagt, bürsten macht die Wolle lebendig! Hast du Zahnseide benutzt? Die Schuldirektorin wird heute mit dir sprechen."

„Guten Tag, Frau Shimata. Hallo, Juni."

„Guten Tag, Frau Nielsen."

„Juni, wir haben entschieden, dass wir dich in die fünfte Klasse heben. Heute noch. Du wirst die vierte Klasse überspringen wie gefällt dir das?"

Augen blinzeln.

„Also lauf hin zum Zimmer von Frau Mader und hol deine Sachen, dann bringe ich dich zur Klasse von Frau Kayler."

„Aber ich kenne *niemand* in der fünften Klasse!" Regina zählt nicht.

„Mach dir keine Sorgen, ich stelle dich den anderen Fünftklässlern vor, du wirst schnell Freunde finden. Frau Kayler hilft dir dabei. Nun Beeilung, wir wollen die Glocke für die erste Stunde nicht verpassen!"

Auf dem Rücken im Sandkasten. Wolken ziehen vorüber. Komisches Gefühl. Keine Eile. Schwebend. Wie im Wasser. Nur trocken. Bzzzzzz. Die Welt ist rund. Ich lebe auf der runden Welt. Drüben spielen die anderen Kinder. Himmel blau. Keine Zeit. Nur Wolken. Nur Wolken da oben schwebend, vorbeiziehend.

In mein Bauch. Aus.

In. Aus.

Erläuterungen zu diesem Text sind auf der Website http://www.junishimata.com/blog/ unter dem Tag *Road Girl* zu finden. Dort gibt es auch Gelegenheit, Fragen zu stellen.

Wenn dir *Road Girl* gefallen hat, würde ich mich über eine ehrlich Empfehlung, z.B. auf Amazon oder Goodreads, sehr freuen. Danke! Vanessa